Disasters

Air Disasters and Deadly Storms

逃出空難風暴

ANN WEIL

English edition, Copyright © 2004 by Saddleback Educational Publishing.
本書英漢版由 Saddleback Educational Publishing 授權出版,僅限於香港、中國大陸、澳門及台灣銷售。

Development: Kent Publishing Services, Inc.
Design and Production: Signature Design Group, Inc.

Photo Credits: cover, pages 13, 16, 23, Bettmann/Corbis; page 18, Hulton-Deutsch Collection; page 31, Paul Thompson/Eye Ubiquitous ; page 91, Jim McDonald/ Corbis; page 117, Jim Zuckerman/Corbis; page 121, AFP/Corbis; page 129, Corbis/ Sygma

書　　名：逃出空難風暴
　　　　　Air Disasters and Deadly Storms
作　　者：Ann Weil
責　　編：黃家麗
封面設計：張　毅
出　　版：商務印書館 (香港) 有限公司
　　　　　香港筲箕灣耀興道 3 號東滙廣場 8 樓
　　　　　http://www.commercialpress.com.hk
發　　行：香港聯合書刊物流有限公司
　　　　　香港新界大埔汀麗路 36 號中華商務印刷大廈 3 字樓
印　　刷：中華商務彩色印刷有限公司
　　　　　香港新界大埔汀麗路 36 號中華商務印刷大廈 14 字樓
版　　次：2012 年 7 月第 1 版第 1 次印刷
　　　　　©2012 商務印書館 (香港) 有限公司
　　　　　ISBN 978 962 07 1967 7
　　　　　Printed in Hong Kong

CONTENTS 目錄

Exercises 練習

Part 2
Deadly Storms 致命風暴

Exercises 練習

Answer Key

English-Chinese Vocabulary List

More to Read

Publisher's Note
出版說明

今年應該不是世界末日，但災難事故幾乎每天都在發生。怎樣用英語講述重大事故，Disasters 閱讀系列提供一個參考。

Disasters 閱讀系列是 Quality English Learning〈優質英語階梯閱讀〉的全新系列，與已推出兩套 16 本的〈*National Geographic* 百科英語階梯閱讀〉異曲同工，同為閱讀真實題材，學好生活英語。

系列分 Level 1 和 Level 2，共五本書，每本書含兩個災難主題，一共十個，包括：火山爆發、森林大火、太空事故、地震、空難、特大風暴、海難、登山遇險、恐怖襲擊、環境危機。用英語講解災難形成的前因後果，簡明扼要，以英漢對照形式，按時序介紹具代表性的災難，比如穿梭機哥倫比亞號如何解體、唐山大地震造成的巨大破壞等。

按主題解釋關鍵詞語，列出相關事實，以地圖標示災難發生的地點。閱讀之餘，可透過多樣化練習題自我測試。附中英對照生詞表，含專有名詞及常用詞語供快速查閱。

"閱讀真實題材，學好生活英語"是為特點。我們衷心希望，本系列能幫助讀者提高英語表達能力。

商務印書館（香港）有限公司

編輯出版部

Usage Note
使用說明

Step 1

閱讀英漢對照的時間軸、重點詞彙、災難發生地點的地圖，概括理解主題。

Step 2

閱讀英語正文，了解災難事故的前因後果，有需要可看生詞、短語中譯，也可查閱中英對照生詞表及常用詞語。

Step 3

做練習題，自我測試英語能力。

Part 1

Air Disasters
空難

1 Introduction
死於交通意外比墜機少

May 6, 1937

The *Hindenburg* airship catches on fire in Lakehurst, New Jersey.

1937 年 5 月 6 日
興登堡號飛船在新澤西州的萊克赫斯特着火。

December 28, 1979

An Air New Zealand airplane crashes into a volcano in Antarctica.

1979 年 12 月 28 日
一架紐西蘭航空公司的航機撞上南極洲一個火山。

Where is Lakehurst? 萊克赫斯特在哪裏？ ▶▶▶

LAKEHURST 萊克赫斯特

DID YOU KNOW? 你知道嗎？

A mechanical failure caused a commercial airplane crash in Chicago in 1979. More people died in this crash than any other single plane crash in the United States.

1979年芝加哥一架商用航機墜毀，這次墜機死亡人數是美國空難中有史以來最多的。

KEY TERMS 重點詞彙

airship - an aircraft filled with gas, not air

飛船是一種填滿氣體而非空氣的飛行器

mechanical failure - a problem in the machinery

機械故障是機器出現的問題

commercial airline - a service that people pay to fly somewhere

商用航班提供付費飛往某處的服務

Chapter One:
Introduction

Flying is a very safe way to travel. More people are killed in car accidents than plane crashes. Yet many people are afraid of flying.

Why is stepping onto a plane scarier than getting into a car? Perhaps it's because flying seems so extraordinary[1]. Anyone who has looked down on[2] clouds from inside a plane knows this feeling.

Perhaps it's because passengers on a plane are helpless when there is a problem in the air. Perhaps it's because many people survive car accidents, but only a lucky few survive a plane crash.

---

1 extraordinany, *adj*：特別的
2 look down on：俯瞰

Before Commercial Airplanes

The *Hindenburg* was a German airship. An airship is like a blimp[1]. It carried passengers across the Atlantic Ocean. The trip took about 65 hours.

The *Hindenburg* flew between Frankfurt, Germany, and Lakehurst[2], New Jersey. It was built in 1936 and flew 186,000 miles safely.

Snapshot

The Hindenburg 興登堡號飛船

1　blimp, *n*：小飛艇
2　Lake hurst：雷克赫斯特

Airships were very different from[1] planes. They could float like a balloon. They were filled with hydrogen instead of air.

Hydrogen explodes and burns when it touches fire. The Germans wanted to use helium gas[2] instead. Helium does not explode or burn.

It would have been safer. But the Germans did not have helium gas. America was the only country that did.

The American government refused to sell helium to the Germans. They were suspicious of[3] Adolf Hitler. This was a few years before World War II began.

So the Germans used hydrogen in their airships, even though they knew it was dangerous.

---

1   different from：異於…
2   helium gas：氦氣
3   suspicious of：懷疑

The Last Trip

The *Hindenburg*'s last trip began in May 1937. It left Frankfurt, Germany with 97 people on board. 36 were passengers. 61 were crew.

When it tried to dock[1] in New Jersey, it caught fire. There was an explosion. A huge ball of flames shot out from the top of the airship. It fell to the ground in a blaze.

A radio announcer was making a live broadcast. There was no TV then. People listened to the radio instead. The announcer[2] was watching as the *Hindenburg* burst into flames.

He was shocked! He tried to describe what happened. But he was so upset, he was crying. "This is the worst thing I've ever witnessed," he said.

1　dock：靠碼頭

2　announcer, *n*：播音員

36 people died. No one wanted to fly in[1] an airship anymore. The other German airships were scrapped[2]. The Germans used the aluminum frames to build airplanes to fight in World War II.

Snapshot

No one knows for sure exactly how the Hindenburg caught fire. The most likely explanation is that a spark of static electricity triggered the explosion.

沒人知道興登堡號飛船是怎樣着火的，最有可能是因靜電火花引發爆炸。

---

1 fly in：乘⋯飛行
2 scrap, v：廢棄

A New Way to Travel

Airplanes were used in World War II. But there were no airline companies in the 1940s. Ordinary people could not simply buy a plane ticket.

The British Overseas Airways Corporation (BOAC) was the first commercial airline. BOAC's first flight was on May 2, 1952.

It went from London, England, to Johannesburg, South Africa. This was the first time passengers paid to fly somewhere.

Exactly one year later, a BOAC[1] plane crashed. The plane was flying over India. It broke up[2] in the air.

There were 43 people on board. Some were passengers. Others were part of the crew. All of them were killed.

---

1 BOAC：英國海外航空公司
2 break up：解體

The First Commercial Airplanes

Snapshot

The first commercial airplanes were called "Comets."

首家商用航機被稱為"彗星"客機。

The first commercial airplanes could carry only about 50 people. Now, hundreds of[1] people can travel together on a single jet. A crash today can be deadlier[2] than ever before.

---

1   hundreds of：許多
2   deadlier：傷亡更嚴重

Why do planes crash?

Planes crash for different reasons. Sometimes bad weather is involved. And pilots can make mistakes.

Sometimes these mistakes are deadly. Sometimes there is a problem with the airplane itself. This is called mechanical failure[1].

A Deadly Error

Air New Zealand offered air tours of Antarctica beginning in 1977. These flights became very popular. Many people wanted to see the area near the South Pole.

A highlight of the flight was a view of Mt. Erebus. Mt. Erebus is a very big volcano.

Flying near the South Pole is difficult and dangerous. The weather is unpredictable[2]. Pilots could not use a regular compass.

---

1   mechanical failure：機件故障
2   unpredictable, *adj*：捉摸不透的

It wouldn't work properly so close to the magnetic pole[1].

Pilots relied on the plane's computer instead. They programmed their route[2] into the computer.

On one flight in 1979, the pilot couldn't see out his window. He wanted to give the passengers a better view of Mt. Erebus. He brought the plane lower so they could see the volcano.

The computer said it would be all right. But the computer was wrong. The program had been entered incorrectly. The plane crashed into Mt. Erebus. All 257 people on board were killed.

---

1   magnetic pole：磁極
2   program sb's route：為某人的路線編寫程式

Mechanical Failure

Mechanical failure was to blame for a crash in Chicago in 1979. The left engine came off seconds before take off. The plane kept going[1].

The pilots could not see what had happened. They didn't realize it was a major emergency.

They tried to turn around and land the plane safely. But there was too much damage to the plane. The plane crashed about 30 seconds after takeoff[2]. It was less than a mile from the end of the runway.

The left wing tip hit the ground. The plane exploded. All 271 people on board died.

---

1   keep going：繼續運行
2   takeoff, *n*：起飛

Pieces of the plane scattered[1] everywhere. Some fell onto a nearby mobile home[2] park. A big fire broke out. Two people on the ground were killed. It was the worst single plane crash in the United States.

---

1   scatter, *v*：散佈
2   mobile home：活動車屋

Snapshot

Firefighters search for bodies in the debris of the American Airlines DC-10. The plane crashed on takeoff from O'Hare International Airport killing all 271 people aboard. Flags mark places where bodies were found. It was the worst air disaster in U.S. history.

消防員在美國航空公司 DC-10 飛機殘骸中搜索遺體，航機從奧黑爾國際機場起飛時墜毀，機上271人死亡。旗子標示找到遺體的位置，這次意外是美國史上最嚴重的空難。

2 Tenerife, 1977
濃霧籠罩中撞機

Timeline 時間軸

March 27, 1977

A bomb explodes in the Las Palmas Airport in the Canary Islands. All flights are sent to an airport in Tenerife.

Two planes collide in the heavy fog at the airport in Tenerife.

1977 年 3 月 27 日

一顆炸彈在加那利羣島上的拉斯帕爾馬斯國際機場爆炸，所有航機被移往特內里費的一個機場。

濃霧籠罩，兩架飛機在特內里費機場相撞。

Where are the Canary Islands? 加那利羣島在哪裏？

CANARY ISLANDS 加那利羣島

KEY TERMS 重點詞彙

terrorism - the use of force to scare people

恐怖手段是用暴力制服他人

taxi - to move along the ground before taking off or after landing

飛機起飛前或着陸後在地面滑行

aviation - the science of flying airplanes

航空學是飛機航行的科學研究

Chapter Two:
Tenerife, 1997

The Canary Islands are near the west coast of North Africa. The islands are popular with tourists. Many Europeans vacation there.

The Canary Islands have two capitals: Santa Cruz and Las Palmas. Las Palmas is located on[1] Grand Canary Island.

A Bomb!

On March 27, 1977, a bomb exploded at Las Palmas airport. Some people were injured. But no one was killed.

However, this act of terrorism had an unexpected and deadly consequence. It set in motion a chain of[2] events. The result was a horrific plane crash on the nearby island of Tenerife.

---

1   locate on：位於…之上
2   a chain of：一連串的

The Las Palmas airport was closed after the bomb exploded. They were afraid there might be a second bomb. Planes were sent to Tenerife instead.

The Tenerife airport became very busy. It was crowded with planes from Las Palmas airport. There were too many planes waiting to take off.

Some planes used the runway to reach the takeoff point. This is very unusual. It turned out[1] to be very dangerous, too.

Fog

It was very foggy. The pilots couldn't see very far. The control tower couldn't see the runway[1] either.

Two planes were taxiing down[2] the runway. The first one was a Dutch KLM 747. It turned to get ready for takeoff.

---

1 runway, *n*：跑道
2 taxi down：滑行

The pilot didn't see that there was another plane on the runway. That plane was a Pan Am 747. The Pan Am pilot had missed a turn-off in the fog.

Disaster!

The KLM pilot thought the control tower had said it was clear to take off. So he zoomed down the runway.

The Pan Am pilot saw the KLM plane coming. He tried to get out of the way. But there wasn't enough time.

The KLM pilot saw the second plane and tried to lift off early. He forced the 747 into the air. The plane got off the ground. But it wasn't high enough to hop over[1] the other 747.

The KLM plane slammed into[2] the side of the Pan Am 747. The landing gear from the KLM plane was ripped off. The KLM plane skidded down the runway for about

---

1   hop over：躍過
2   slam into：猛烈撞擊

1,000 feet. Then it burst into flames.

The Pan Am plane's upstairs first class lounge was smashed off[1]. Some Pan Am passengers thought a bomb had exploded. The crash also left openings[2] in the side of the Pan Am 747.

Some people were able to climb out through these holes. They jumped down onto the grass next to the runway.

The pilot and some of the crew also escaped. They were lucky they could get out so quickly. The Pan Am's engine was still running.

There was a fire under the wing. Both planes were full of fuel. Explosions rocked the Pan Am plane. Then the second plane also burst into flames.

The fog was so bad, the control tower didn't see what had happened. But they heard the explosions.

---

1   smash off：粉碎
2   opening, *n*：缺口

At first, no one was sure what was going on. Some thought a fuel tank had exploded. Perhaps the terrorists had struck again. Then they received reports that there was a fire.

The fire trucks[1] found the KLM plane first. It was completely on fire. There were no survivors. Then they realized another plane was also on fire[2].

70 people from the Pan Am plane escaped. But nine of these died later in the hospital. That brought the total number of dead to 583.

The fires burned till the afternoon of the next day. By then it was clear that this was the worst disaster in aviation history up until that time. And it all happened on the ground.

---

1 fire truck, *n*：救火車
2 on fire：起火

Snapshot

Worst Disaster in Aviation History

航空史上最嚴重的空難

Worst Fire On Board an Airplane: Riyadh, Saudi Arabia, 1980

Many air disasters happen very fast. The pilot does not have time to save the plane and people on board. But an air disaster in 1980 could have been prevented if only the pilot had acted quickly.

A fire broke out on a plane about six minutes after it took off. It was in the cargo area[1] where the luggage is stored. The pilot knew there was a fire. He could have requested an emergency landing[2]. That way the fire equipment would be waiting on the runway. The fire could have been put out right away. Passengers could

---

1   cargo area：貨運區
2   emergency landing：緊急降落

have left the plane immediately using the emergency slides[1]. But the pilot decided not to do this.

Instead, he landed normally. Perhaps he did not realize the fire was so serious. The plane touched down safely back at the airport. But the pilot did not stop the plane immediately. He taxied slowly down the runway before stopping.

This added to[2] the delay in putting out the fire. It took a full 23 minutes after touchdown before the doors were opened. By this time it was too late.

---

1   emergency slide：緊急逃生滑梯
2   add to：加劇

The fire spread to the main cabin. It blazed through the passenger area. Smoke and fire killed everyone on board. 287 passengers and 14 crew died.

Fifteen of the passengers were infants[1]. These lives could have been saved if the pilot had acted properly. His mistake had tragic results[2].

---

1   infant：嬰孩
2   tragic result：悲劇後果

3 Chile, 1972
吃死人的肉保命

Timeline 時間軸

October 13, 1972

An airplane carrying a Uruguayan rugby team crashes in the Andes Mountains.

1972 年 10 月 13 日
一架載着烏拉圭橄欖球球隊的航機撞上安第斯山脈。

December 22, 1972

The survivors of the crash are rescued.

1972 年 12 月 22 日
撞機事故的生還者被救出。

Where are the Andes Mountains? 安第斯山脈在哪裏？

ANDES MOUNTAINS 安第斯山脈

DID YOU KNOW? 你知道嗎？

In 1993, the story of the Andes Mountains plane crash was made into a movie called *Alive*.

1993年安第斯山脈撞機的故事，被拍成電影"我們要活着回去"。

KEY TERMS 重點詞彙

ordeal - a difficult experience

苦難、嚴峻的考驗

turbulence - winds that cause an airplane to shake in the air

湍流使航機在空中搖晃

severed - cut off 切斷

cannibalism - the practice of humans eating human flesh

人的同類相食

Chapter three:
Chile, 1972

Surviving a plane crash is lucky. But it can also be the beginning of a more difficult struggle. Sometimes planes crash in remote areas.

Imagine being stuck on a snowy mountaintop[1]. You survived the plane crash. But some of your friends and family did not. It is icy cold at night.

You're afraid you'll freeze to death in your sleep. Worst of all, there's nothing to eat.

This is what happened to a group of South American Rugby players and their families. They chartered[2] an airplane. They wanted to go from Uruguay to Chile.

---

1   mountaintop, *n*：山頂
2   charter, *v*：租

They expected their flight to last about 3.5 hours. But their plane crashed into the Andes Mountains. Their ordeal[1] lasted 72 days.

Fun and Games

The plane left Carasco airport in Uruguay. The first hours of the flight were uneventful. Most of the players were in their late teens and early twenties. They talked about rugby. Some played cards. Others read books.

Then weather turned bad. The pilot decided not to fly across the Andes that day. Instead they stopped in Mendoza, Argentina. They stayed there overnight.

The next day, they took off from[2] Mendoza. It was Friday the 13th of October 1972. The players were eager to go. But the pilot was worried.

1　ordeal：苦難
2　take off from：以⋯為出發點

Was it safe to cross the mountains? He couldn't stay another day in Argentina. He was flying a Uruguayan military plane. They were not allowed to stay in Argentina for more than one day.

Flying over the Andes is challenging. The weather can change suddenly. Some of the mountains are very tall. They are too high to fly over[1]. So planes fly through mountain passes.

Many planes make the trip safely. They use modern equipment. The military plane was equipped with the latest instruments. The pilot decided to fly through one of the passes. They lifted off[2] at about 3:30.

The players were in a good mood. They were tossing a ball around the cabin. Shortly after takeoff, the plane hit some turbulence.

---

1 fly over：飛到另一個地方去
2 lift off：起飛

The plane began to shake. It was a very rough flight. Many of the passengers were scared. But much worse was yet to come.

Flying Blind

At first there was a good tail wind[1]. This meant the wind was blowing in the same direction the plane was travelling. This made the plane go faster.

But the wind changed. It turned into a strong head wind. That meant the wind was hitting the plane head-on[2]. This slowed the plane down.

But the pilot and co-pilot were not paying attention to the wind conditions. They thought they were still travelling as fast as they were at the start.

It was cloudy. They couldn't see out the window. They didn't use the equipment properly. They were flying blind. And they

---

1   tail wind：順風
2   head-on, *adv*：迎面地

were already way off course[1].

The pilot radioed the Santiago airport. They thought they were almost ready to come down into the airport. In fact, they were still in the mountains.

The controller in Santiago did not confirm where the plane was. He just took the pilot's word.

The pilot brought the plane down. They came out below the clouds. The pilot expected to see flat, green fields. Instead he saw sharp peaks and ridges[2].

The passengers saw this, too. The snowy mountains were just 10 feet from the window!

The pilot tried to save the plane. But he couldn't get the plane to climb fast enough. The engines screamed. Many of the passengers began to pray.

---

1   off course：偏離航向
2   ridge, *n*：山脊

For some of them, these were their last moments alive.

Crash!

The plane crashed into the side of a mountain. One of the wings was ripped off. The severed[1] wing cut off the tail.

Five people were sucked out instantly. They were still strapped in their seats. The plane bounced over rocks.

The other wing was snapped off[2]. The wingless plane shot forward. It flew through the air like a torpedo. Then it landed smoothly onto the snowy mountainside.

But it didn't come to a stop. It slid down the mountain at great speed. Two more people were sucked out from a hole at the back.

---

1 severed：切斷的
2 snap off：折斷

Finally, what was left of the plane stopped at a huge snow bank. The crash was over. But for the survivors, the struggle to stay alive was just beginning.

Staying Alive

Roberto Canessa was one of the surviving rugby players. He was a medical student. There was no First Aid equipment. But Roberto still managed to treat many injuries.

The captain of the rugby team also survived. His name was Marcelo Perez. Marcelo organized people to look through the wreckage[1] for things they could use.

They tried the radio. But it didn't work. The batteries were in the tail. And the tail was long gone.

It started to snow. It was already dark by 6 o'clock in the evening. They used the seat covers[2] like blankets. If they hadn't,

---

1 wreckage, *n*：殘片
2 seat cover, *n*：座椅套

they would have died from the cold. At night, the temperature fell way below freezing.

They figured out a way to melt snow for drinking water. They used aluminum sheets from the plane. The sun warmed the metal.

But food was a problem. There wasn't much. Some of the players had brought chocolate. There were also some crackers and nuts and a few other things.

Days passed. Planes flew over. But no help appeared. The planes flying overhead[1] could not see the plane below. The roof of the plane was painted white. It blended in[2] with the snowy mountainside. It was invisible from the air.

Another player, Nando Parrado, was knocked unconscious when the plane crashed. When he woke up, he heard some very bad news.

---

1 overhead, *adv*：在空中
2 blend in：與…和諧

Roberto told him that his mother had died in the crash. His sister was barely hanging onto life[1]. Nando tried to keep his sister warm. But she died, too.

Bad weather kept them huddled[2] inside for days. An avalanche had smashed their shelter. Several of the surviving players were killed, including the team captain, Marcelo Perez. Still, no help had arrived.

They ran out of food. Cannibalism was their only hope of survival. They were all very religious. This made their only option even more difficult. But they couldn't survive without food. Their will to survive was very strong. They made their decision to stay alive.

---

1 hang onto life：掙扎求存
2 huddle, v：蜷縮身體

Rescue

Weeks passed. Nando decided he would walk off[1] the mountain. He would go for help, himself. Roberto Canessa went with him.

The two young men walked for 10 days. Eventually[2], they came to a village. The next day, a helicopter took Nando back to the plane. Help finally arrived 72 days after the crash. Of the 45 people on board, only 16 survived.

---

1 walk off：離開
2 eventually, *adv*：最終

4 Washington D.C., 1982

捨身救人的勇者

Timeline 時間軸

January 13, 1982

An airplane hits a bridge then plunges into the Potomac River in Washington, D. C.

1982 年 1 月 13 日

一架飛機撞橋後插入首都華盛頓的波拖馬可河裏。

April 2, 1982

The Falklands War begins.

1982 年 4 月 2 日

福克蘭羣島戰爭爆發。

Where is Washington, D.C.？首都華盛頓在哪裏？

WASHINGTON, D.C. 華盛頓

DID YOU KNOW? 你知道嗎？

A brave survivor of the crash in D.C. helped save other people. He died before he was rescued himself.

在首都特區有一個勇敢的生還者，為着拯救別人犧牲自己生命。

KEY TERMS 重點詞彙

visibility - how clearly things can be seen

視程是能看清事物的能力

commuter - a person who travels daily between home and work

通勤者指每天來回於住所和工作地方的人

flight attendant - a person who looks after the passengers on an airplane

飛行服務員負責在航機上照顧乘客

lifeline - a rope used to save a person in the water

救生索即拋落水中救人的繩索

Chapter Four:
Washington, D. C., 1982

Bad weather makes flying more dangerous. However, it is rarely the only reason for a crash.

Planes are equipped[1] to fly through clouds and most storms. Pilots are trained to handle difficult situations. Airports can usually continue to operate safely, no matter what[2] the weather.

Unfortunately, bad weather and pilot error can be a deadly combination.

Snow and Ice

The winter of 1982 was bitter cold. Flying to Florida seemed a great way to escape the freezing temperatures. On January 13th, many people in Washington, D.C. were doing just that.

---

1   equip, *v*：裝備
2   no matter what：無論甚麼

The city's National Airport was full of people in search of warmer weather down south. It was snowing in Washington, D.C. that day. Snow piled up[1] on the runways.

The airport closed so the runways could be ploughed[2]. It took about an hour and a half to clear away the snow. No planes could take off during this time. This made a lot of flights late.

The airport reopened. Planes were lined up for takeoff. One of them was bound for Fort Lauderdale, Florida. There were 74 passengers on board.

Visibility was poor. The temperature was below freezing. The airport was behind schedule. Planes were waiting to land. The control tower did not want more delays. Flight 90 to Fort Lauderdale was cleared for takeoff.

---

1 pile up：堆積
2 plough, v：翻起；美式拼法是 plow

Crash

Flight 90 never made it to Florida. Less than a minute after takeoff, Flight 90 was already in serious trouble. The 737 dipped down[1] onto a bridge over the Potomac River.

This is a busy commuter route. Traffic was moving very slowly because of the snow. The plane skimmed over[2] the road. It smashed into six cars and a truck. It tore off a large section of railing. Then the plane broke in two and plunged into the icy river.

Rescue

Both pieces of the plane started to sink. Rescue boats could not reach the plane. There was too much ice on the river. It took twenty minutes for a rescue helicopter to get there.

---

1 dip down：落下
2 skim over：滑過

By then, the people in the front part of the plane had all died. Some passengers who had been seated at the rear had struggled free of the wreckage. They were hanging on to pieces of ice in the freezing water.

Many people watched the dramatic[1] rescue on television. The helicopter lifted five people out—four passengers and one flight attendant.

They were the only survivors. The crash also killed four people on the bridge.

A Hero Dies

One of the passengers chose to help others instead of saving himself. He was in the icy river with the other survivors.

The helicopter dropped life vests[2]. The man passed them to other people. The helicopter lowered a lifeline. This could drag people to safety. Twice, the man

---

1 dramatic, *adj*：激動人心的
2 vest, *n*：背心

handed the lifeline to other survivors.

He could have been lifted out himself. When the helicopter came back for him, he was gone.

What really happened?

The most obvious cause for this crash was the cold weather. Ice can build up on the plane. All that ice adds to the weight of the plane and its load of people and luggage. An icy plane can't climb as fast.

Airports have special machines to melt the ice. Flight 90 used this equipment. But an hour passed after the plane was de-iced[1].

All the evidence pointed to[2] icing as the cause of the crash. But this was not the whole story.

---

1   de-iced, *adj*：除冰的
2   point to：顯示真相

The investigation showed something else. The engines were not operating fully. Sometimes slush[1] can get inside the engine itself. The engines will still work. But they will not work as well.

The 737 had engine anti-icing[2] equipment. This would have solved the problem. But the crew did not turn it on! Their mistake along with the icy weather caused the crash.

---

1 slush, *n*：半融雪
2 anti-icing：防冰

5 Shot Down
珍寶客機遭導彈擊落

Timeline 時間軸

September 1, 1983
A Korean Airlines commercial plane is shot down over the former Soviet Union.

1983 年 9 月 1 日
一架大韓航空的商用航機在前蘇聯上空遭擊落。

March 12 – 13, 1993
An Iran Air commercial plane is shot down in the Persian Gulf.

1993 年 3 月 12 – 13 日
一部伊朗航空公司的商用飛機遭擊落，跌進波斯灣。

Where is Persian Gulf? 波斯灣在哪裏？ ▶▶▶

PERSIAN GULF 波斯灣

DID YOU KNOW? 你知道嗎？

The Korean Airlines plane was about 300 miles off course when it was shot down.

大韓航空的飛機遭擊落時，偏離航線300英里。

KEY TERMS 重點詞彙

jumbo jet - a large jet plane

珍寶客機是大型噴氣式航機

airbus - a short- or medium-range plane

空中巴士指短程或中程航機

high alert - very watchful, often because there is danger

因看見有危險而提高警覺

Chapter Five:
Shot Down

Shooting at planes is common during wartime. However, passenger planes are rarely military targets. Still, two jumbo jets were shot down in the 1980s.

Both were shot down by major powers: the first by the Russians and the second by the Americans. Both were mistakes. Unfortunately, they were very deadly mistakes[1].

Korean Airlines, 1983

Passenger planes are supposed to stay on certain flight paths. These paths are like imaginary roads in the sky. In 1983, a Korean Airlines 747 strayed from[2] its flight path.

---

1   deadly mistake：致命錯誤
2   stray from：偏離

The plane was flying from Alaska to South Korea. But it was about 300 miles off course. The 747 flew over secret missile test sites in the former Soviet Union.

The Russians thought it was a spy plane. A Soviet fighter plane fired an air-to-air missile at the 747. The missile[1] hit its target.

The 747 crashed into the Sea of Japan. There were 269 people on board the 747. All of them were killed. Other countries were very angry and upset. They blamed the Russians for killing innocent people.

The United States was one of the loudest voices against the Russians. One of the passengers on board the 747 was a United States Congressman[2]. Later, the Russians admitted they had made a mistake.

The 747 was not a spy plane. But no one knows why the plane was so far off course. Maybe the plane's computer was broken.

---

1 missile, *n*：導彈
2 congressman, *n*：國會議員

Or perhaps the pilot was taking a shortcut to save fuel. It is still a mystery. And it will probably never be solved.

Iran Air, 1988

Five years later, the United States government did almost the same thing. An American warship shot down an Iran Air airbus. They thought it was a military plane about to attack them.

The warship was in the Persian Gulf. It was a tense situation. An Iraqi missile hit another ship and killed 37 sailors. The Americans were on high alert[1].

They expected another attack. They warned all airplanes and helicopters to stay far away from U. S. warships. But there was a flight path near one U. S. Navy warship[2]. The ship was named the *Vincennes*.

---

1   on high alert：提高警惕
2   warship, *n*：軍艦

Radar operators on the *Vincennes* reported an airplane coming toward them. A regular passenger airplane will climb steadily during takeoff. But this plane was coming fast toward them.

The captain thought the ship was under attack[1]. The target was shot down.

But it wasn't a fighter plane[2]. It was a regular passenger plane. The radar operators had made a mistake. 290 people were on board. All were killed.

The Navy admitted it was a tragic accident. The American government eventually paid $62 million to the victims' families.

1　under attack：受到攻擊
2　fighter plane：戰機

6 Terrorism in the Air

雙子大廈被飛機撞毀

Timeline 時間軸

September 11, 2001
Two hijacked planes crash into the World Trade Centre in New York City.

2001 年 9 月 11 日
兩架被劫持的航機撞向世界貿易中心。

September 11, 2001
A hijacked plane crashes into the Pentagon in Washington, D. C.

2001 年 9 月 11 日
一架被劫持的航機撞落首都華盛頓的五角大廈。

Where is New York City? 紐約市在哪裏？ ▶▶▶▶

NEW YORK CITY 紐約市

DID YOU KNOW? 你知道嗎？

Most officials believe Osama bin Laden led the terrorist attacks. The Airline Pilots Association and the Air Transport Association offered a $2 million reward for his arrest.

多數官員相信拉登發動恐怖襲擊，航空公司飛行員協會和航空運輸協會為緝捕他懸賞200萬美元。

KEY TERMS 重點詞彙

hijack - to take over by force and redirect
劫持是以武力接管並重新導向

air traffic - presence of aircraft in the sky
空中交通指航機在空中的航行

twin towers - two 110-storey skyscrapers, together called the World Trade Center
雙子塔為兩棟110層高的摩天大廈，合稱世界貿易中心

the Pentagon - headquarters of the Department of Defence
五角大廈即美國國防部總部的所在

Chapter Six:
Terrorism in the Air

Most air disasters are accidents. Unfortunately, some are planned. Occasionally people hijack planes. Some of the most horrific air disasters are acts of terrorism.

September 11, 2001

The morning of September 11th was a usual busy weekday morning at American airports. But that day turned into a nightmare[1] when four planes were hijacked.

Two planes crashed into[2] the twin towers of the World Trade Centre in New York City. Another hijacked plane crashed into the Pentagon in Washington, D. C.

---

1   turn into a nightmare：變成惡夢
2   crash into：撞進

The fourth hijacked plane crashed near Pittsburgh, Pennsylvania. That plane was probably headed for[1] the White House, Camp David, or the U. S. Capitol building[2].

But brave passengers aboard the flight stopped the hijackers from hitting their intended target. Everyone on all four hijacked planes was killed. Thousands of people in the twin towers of the World Trade Centre were killed, too.

About 180 people died at the Pentagon. It was the worst air disaster ever. And it was the worst terrorist attack on American soil.

The Twin Towers Fall

The first plane crashed into the north tower at about 8:45 a.m. It tore a huge hole in the side of the building. Then it exploded.

1 　head for：朝⋯進發
2 　U.S. Capitol building：美國國會大廈

The second plane slammed into the south tower about 15 minutes later. Both planes were full of jet fuel. The fuel started huge fires. The towers started to crumble[1]. Many people escaped. They got out just in time[2].

At 10:05 a.m., the south tower collapsed. Then the north tower collapsed a little more than 20 minutes later.

Almost 3,000 people died at the World Trade Centre that morning. Hundreds of the victims were firefighters and police. They had arrived at the scene to help. They were trying to save people when the towers collapsed.

The Pentagon

At 9:43 a.m., another hijacked plane crashed into the Pentagon building in Arlington, Virginia. The Pentagon is

---

1 crumble, *v*：碎成細屑
2 in time：及時

the headquarters[1] for the Department of Defence[2].

It contains offices for the Army, Navy and Air Force. About 23,000 people work at the Pentagon. Everyone on board the plane was killed. So were about 120 people who worked at the Pentagon.

Grounded

All the New York City airports were closed just after the attacks on the World Trade Centre. Less than half an hour later, all airports in the country were closed. Planes that were in the air had to land at the nearest airport. There was no air traffic[3] in the entire United States. For the first time ever since jet travel began, there were no planes in the sky over America.

---

1 headquarter, *n*：總部
2 the Department of Defence：國防部
3 air traffic：航空交通

7 Lower the number of accidents
減少飛行意外

The Federal Aviation[1] Administration (FAA) is a part of the U.S. government. The FAA makes sure that travel by plane is as safe as it can be.

In 1998, the FAA started a project called Safer Skies. Safer Skies aims to lower the number of deaths caused by aviation accidents by the year 2007. Three teams work together[2] in this program.

One of the teams is called the Commercial Aviation Safety Team (CAST). CAST hopes to lower the number of commercial aviation accidents by 80 percent. They look into problems that cause the greatest number of deaths. These problems include engine failure, loss of control, and weather.

1　aviation, *n*：航空
2　work together：共同合作

Exercises 練習

1 Vocabulary 詞彙

1.1 Word Ladders 字梯

按提示改詞語的一個字母，使它變成下一個詞語，
請見示範。

topmost body part	head
what a doctor does	hea**l**
greenish-blue colour	**t**eal
to say	_____
not short	_____
an animal's extension	tail

low clouds	fog
an enemy	fo**e**
a female deer	_____
to colour	_____
"yes" to a ship captain	_____
card that stands for one	_____
frozen water	ice

fuel for cars	gas
owns	**h**as
belonging to him	_____
bro's opposite (bro = brother)	_____
polite address for a man	_____
a mixture of gases	air

cannot see	blind
dull or flavourless	bland
a product line	_____
fibres in food such as cereal	_____
a type of vegetable	_____
birds' mouths	_____
mountaintops	peaks

1.2 Making Connections 聯想

選擇互有關聯的一對詞語，然後用英語描述兩者關係。請見示範。

head — tail   fog — ice   gas — air   blind — peaks

e.g. Head and Tail can both relate to wind direction.

_____

_____

_____

2 Initial Understanding 初步理解

2.1 Read for Details 細讀

回答以下問題，答案前加上章節。請見示範。

Ch 1 1. When were people first able to buy a plane ticket?

　　People could first buy a plane ticket in 1952.

_____

_____ 2. What do pilots use when they cannot see?

_____

_____ 3. How can a plane be de-iced?

_____

_____ 4. When was the only time since commercial flights began no planes flew over the U.S. and why?

_____

_____ 5. What deadly "air disaster" actually happened on the ground?

_____

_____ 6. What might have made the Hindenburg safe from fire?

_____

_____7. Why couldn't other planes see the plane that crashed on a mountain in Chile?

_____

_____ 8. Why did the Soviets and the U. S. think the passenger planes were spy planes?

_____

_____ 9. How were the stranded survivors in Chile finally rescued?

_____

_____ 10. How were survivors rescued from the Potomac River in Washington, D. C.?

_____

3 Interpretation 解釋

3.1 Flow Charts 流程圖

流程圖顯示一連串事件，循箭號方向讀去，看事情怎樣發生。請見示範。

根據本書的關鍵事件，完成整個流程圖。

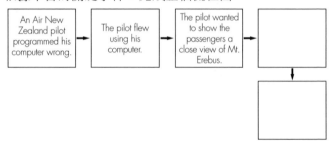

3.2 Sequence of Events 事件發展

以下是表示順序的連接詞：

first, then, next, last, second, finally, afterwards, before

參考上一題流程圖的內容加上表示順序的連接詞，另寫一段文字。請見首兩句的示範。

The left engine came off a plane in Chicago right <u>before</u> take-off. <u>Then</u> the pilot tried to go back and land <u>after</u> take-off.

Part 2

Deadly Storms
致命風暴

1 Introduction
致命暴風雨捲土重來

Timeline 時間軸

September 12, 1988
Hurricane Gilbert strikes Jamaica with 125 mph gusts of wind.

1988 年 9 月 12 日
颶風吉伯特以風速每小時 125 英里侵襲牙買加。

December 27, 1998
A storm hits sailors in the Sydney to Hobart yacht race. Waves more than 80 feet high sweep sailors into the sea.

1998 年 12 月 27 日
荷巴特帆船比賽遭遇風暴，殃及一眾船員。浪高 80 英尺，把船員掃入海中。

Where is Jamaica? 牙買加在哪裏？

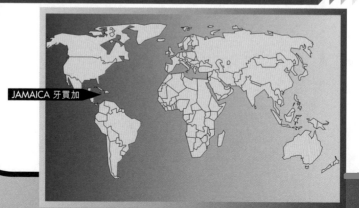

JAMAICA 牙買加

DID YOU KNOW? 你知道嗎？

Hurricanes have at least 74 mph winds. If the winds are under 74 mph, the hurricane is considered a tropical storm.

颶風風力最少可達每小時74英里，若風力少於每小時74英里被視作熱帶風暴。

KEY TERMS 重點詞彙

meteorologist - a scientist who studies the weather

氣象學者是研究天氣的科學家

tropical cyclone - a severe tropical storm with strong winds moving around a low-pressure centre

熱帶氣旋指圍着低壓中心旋轉的強烈熱帶風暴

storm surge - a mountain of water that occurs when a storm sucks up water from the ocean

風暴潮是風暴吸掉海水後，引致大水傾流

Chapter One:
Introduction

Bad weather happens all the time. Rain may spoil a picnic or ball game. Or it may be too cold and icy to play outside. Thunder and lightning can be frightening.

Most of the time, bad weather is just annoying. Sometimes, though, bad weather can be dangerous.

Storms can be killers. Many natural disasters are caused by bad weather. Strong winds can tear roofs off houses.

Trees can be ripped[1] from the ground and tossed into[2] the air. Cars and buses may be blown off the road. Heavy rains cause flooding. Bad floods can wash away entire villages. A storm at sea puts boats and sailors at risk.

---

1   rip, v：扯破
2   toss into：扔進

Watching the Weather

Scientists who study the weather are called meteorologists[1]. Many of them use computers and pictures from outer space to do their job.

They track storms and share their information with each other. Meteorologists can't control the weather, but they can often tell when and where a storm will strike.

Many people listen to weather reports on the radio. Television news programs include reports on the weather, too. Weather reports can be lifesavers[2]. They warn people of bad storms heading their way. This gives people time to go somewhere safe to wait out the storm.

1　meteorologist, *n*：氣象學家
2　lifesaver, *n*：救生者

Tropical Storms

Tropical storms kill many thousands of people all over the world. These powerful storms begin in the warm ocean waters near the equator[1]. The most severe tropical storms are called tropical cyclones.

Most tropical storms stay out at sea. Boats and ships may be at risk from these storms, but in general they cause very little damage. However, when a strong tropical storm strikes land, it can be a disaster.

Huge waves crash onto the shore. The storm sucks up[2] water from the ocean. This mountain of water is called a storm surge. When the storm hits land, it brings this water with it. A storm surge can flood land near the coast. This is often the storm's biggest killer.

1　equator, *n*：赤道
2　suck up：吸取

Meteorologists track tropical storms. They predict where the storm will go. Sometimes the storm changes course and strikes where no one expected. But most of the time, people have some warning before a tropical storm hits land.

Some storms strike with little or no warning. Tornadoes are nature's most violent spinning storms. They have the fastest winds on Earth. Winds inside a tornado can whip around[1] at 300 mph.

Tornadoes form inside thunderclouds. Then they dip down from the sky toward land. When a tornado touches down, it can cause tremendous damage.

A tornado is like a giant vacuum cleaner. It sucks up everything in its path. Houses, cars, people, and animals can all be pulled into[2] the tornado.

The powerful winds rip things apart. Broken glass, wood, and metal whirl

---

1 whip around：轉過身來
2 pull into：進入

inside the tornado.

Most tornadoes do not last very long. Many disappear after only a few minutes. However, some can last for several hours.

Snow and Ice

Blizzards[1] bury cars under hills of snow. Roofs can collapse under the weight of all that snow. People can be stuck in[2] their homes with no way to leave. Icy roads make driving dangerous. Roads may be closed because it is not safe to drive.

Ice storms can bring down power lines. These wires can be deadly if someone accidentally touches them. Homes may be without electricity for days.

People can go without running water and heat. Their stoves and refrigerators don't work without electricity.

---

1   blizzard, *n*：暴風雪
2   stuck in：陷入

After the Storm

Large storms can do a lot of damage. It can take a long time to clean up[1] after a storm.

First, rescue workers help survivors. Saving lives is the number one priority. People may be left homeless from the storm. They need food, water, and a new place to live. Then, power and phone lines need to be fixed. Roads must be cleared. Workers repair buildings and bridges.

Eventually, life returns to[2] normal, until the next deadly storm hits.

---

1 clean up：清理
2 return to：恢復

Snapshot

Earth is not the only planet that has storms. Satellite photos show a storm like a hurricane on Jupiter. Scientists believe this storm has gone on for hundreds of years.

地球並非唯一一個能產生風暴的行星，衛星圖片顯示木星上產生的旋風，科學家相信這場風暴已持續百年未散。

Hurricanes, Typhoons, and Cyclones

Hurricanes are tropical cyclones[1]. Typhoons are also tropical cyclones. They are basically the same. The main difference between the two types is where they start. Hurricanes form in the Atlantic Ocean and the Caribbean[2]. Typhoons begin in the Pacific Ocean. Storms beginning in the Indian Ocean are simply called cyclones.

---

1   tropical cyclone：熱帶氣旋
2   the Caribbean：加勒比海

2 Cyclones
大旋風導致嚴重傷亡

November 13, 1970

A cyclone kills 500,000 people when it strikes the Ganges region.

1970 年 11 月 13 日
大旋風侵襲恆河地區，害了 500,000 條人命。

April 29, 1991

A cyclone strikes Bangladesh and 250,000 die.

1991 年 4 月 29 日
大旋風突襲孟加拉，250,000 人喪生。

Where is Bangladesh? 孟加拉在哪裏？ ▶▶▶

BANGLADESH 孟加拉

KEY TERMS 重點詞彙

cyclone - a severe tropical storm that begins in the Indian Ocean

大旋風是發生在印度洋的猛烈熱帶風暴

Ganges region - the area near the Ganges River

恆河地區指靠近恆河一帶的地方

cyclone shelter - a building raised high off the ground to avoid flood waters

大旋風庇護站是距離地面較高的建築物，目的是避免水淹

Chapter Two:
Cyclones

Bad storms can strike any place, any time, but some places in the world have more deadly storms than others.

Cyclones

Cyclones form in the Indian Ocean. Storm surges[1] from these severe tropical storms flood an area near the mouth of the Ganges River.

Bangladesh is a country in southern Asia. It is a very poor country. About 100 million people live in Bangladesh. Many of them struggle[2] to feed themselves and their families.

The best place for them to grow food crops is near the Ganges River.

---

1   surge, v：奔湧向前
2   struggle, v：拼博

Storm surges and rains from tropical storms can cause serious flooding along river areas. Millions of people live along the banks of the Ganges River. Their lives are all at risk[1] when a powerful cyclone strikes.

500,000 Die in 1970 Cyclone

One of the world's worst natural disasters happened in 1970. A powerful cyclone struck the Ganges region. The storm surge swept away[2] homes and people.

Crops were destroyed. Millions of people were left homeless. There was no food to eat. Dead animals polluted the water. There was no clean water to drink. People who had survived the storm surge starved to death[3]. Others got very sick from drinking the dirty water.

---

1   at risk：有危險
2   sweep away：一掃而空
3   starve to death：餓死

The Ganges region suffered many other cyclones. In 1985, water from a storm surge carried away homes and crops. Then, in 1991, there was a cyclone even more powerful than the one in 1970.

140,000 Die in 1991 Cyclone

The cyclone of 1991 killed almost 140,000 people. There were warnings before this cyclone hit. But many people did not have radios or televisions. They did not hear the warnings.

Other people did not believe the warnings. There had been other warnings and no cyclones had hit. They thought this was just another false alarm[1]. But it wasn't.

This cyclone left about 10 million people homeless[2]. Once again, there was no food or clean water to drink. People got very sick. Many died from starvation and disease.

---

1   false alarm：虛報
2   homeless, *adj*：無家可歸的

Preparing for the Next Disaster

The people of Bangladesh must live with[1] the threat of cyclones. They have built many large cyclone shelters to help more people survive these deadly storms. These shelters are special buildings raised[2] high off the ground. People inside the shelters are above the flood waters.

---

1 live with：容忍
2 ...raised：加高

Calcutta, India, 1737

About 300,000 died when a cyclone storm surge hit[1] the Calcutta region of India.

Darwin, Australia, 1974

Cyclone Tracy struck Darwin, Australia early Christmas morning, 1974. It almost destroyed the whole town. Only a few buildings were left standing[2].

---

1 hit, *v*：襲擊
2 be left standing：沒倒塌

Snapshot

Cyclone damage 大旋風造成的損害

3 Hurricanes
颶風摧毀城市

September 21, 1938

A surprise hurricane strikes the northeastern United States.

1938 年 9 月 21 日
一個令人吃驚的颶風侵襲美國的東北部。

October 29, 1998

Hurricane Mitch strikes Central America.

1998 年 10 月 29 日
颶風米奇侵襲中美洲。

Where is Central America? 中美洲在哪裏？

CENTRAL AMERICA 中美洲

KEY TERMS 重點詞彙

hurricane - a tropical storm that begins in the Atlantic Ocean or Caribbean

一種熱帶風暴，形成於大西洋或加勒比海

eye - the centre of the hurricane

颶風眼圍在颶風的中間

mudslide - a huge amount of mud and rocks, which rolls rapidly down a hill

大量沿山坡急瀉的泥石

Chapter Three:
Hurricanes

Thunderclouds block the sun[1]. Heavy rains pour from the sky, hour after hour. Violent winds bend trees to the breaking point and beyond. This is no ordinary thunderstorm. It's a hurricane.

Hurricanes are much more powerful than ordinary thunderstorms[2]. They form in warm, tropical oceans. Most hurricanes stay out at sea. Some hurricanes touch land. These can cause tremendous damage.

Huge waves can wash away houses—and people—too close to the shore. Strong winds tear trees out of the ground and blow cars off the road.

1　block the sun：擋住太陽
2　thunderstorm, *n*：雷暴

A mighty hurricane can flatten a whole town. Many people have been killed by hurricanes.

Inside a Hurricane

A hurricane has winds of at least 74 mph. These winds spin around[1] the "eye," or centre, of the storm.

The eye can be many miles wide. It is calm and quiet. The sky may be clear over the eye, too. People may think the storm has ended when the eye of the storm is passing over[2] them.

This can be a deadly mistake. It is very dangerous to go out in the eye of the storm. The winds that whip around the eye are the most powerful of the storm.

---

1 spin around：圍繞⋯旋轉
2 pass over：經過

Snapshot

A satellite view of a hurricane with the "eye" in the centre.

颶風中心有"風眼"的衛星照片

Galveston[1], Texas, 1900

Galveston, Texas, is an island. It is connected to[2] the rest of Texas by a bridge. Galveston has beautiful beaches. Many people enjoy vacations there.

On September 8, 1900, this pretty city was hit hard by a hurricane. Waves smashed[3] the beaches. A 20-foot storm surge flooded the city.

The bridge was covered with water. People were trapped on the island as the water level continued to rise. Many people drowned.

The hurricane blew at about 115 mph. Water washed away the sand underneath the buildings. Houses collapsed.

About 6,000 people died in Galveston. Thousands more were killed by the same storm when it hit other islands and the mainland.

---

1 Galveston：加爾維斯敦
2 be connected to：相連
3 smash, v：搗碎

In Galveston, about 3,600 homes were lost. This left 10,000 people homeless[1]. The city was destroyed.

A new Galveston was built. This time, there was a sea wall to help protect the city—and the people who lived there—from future storm surges.

The Great Hurricane of 1938

Some places have very few hurricanes. People who live there don't think these powerful storms will cause problems for them.

Unfortunately, some deadly storms strike where they are not expected. They catch people by surprise[2]. This is what happened to people who lived in the northeastern part of the United States in 1938.

1　leave sb homeless：令人無家可歸
2　catch sb by surprise：使人吃驚

Snapshot

Mobile home park destroyed by a hurricane

流動屋場遭颶風摧毀

This part of America hadn't seen a hurricane for many, many years. But a tropical storm was gathering speed in the Bahamas[1].

People expected the storm to blow out to sea. Instead it sped toward land. The hurricane struck land at Long Island, New York, on September 21, 1938. People there were not prepared. There had been no warnings.

The storm blew across Long Island to Connecticut and Rhode Island. It was a strong hurricane with wind gusts[2] of 150 mph.

A 20-foot storm surge swept the coast. 30-foot waves smashed against homes along the beaches. The storm also brought heavy rains to the whole Northeast. This added to the flooding caused by the storm surge.

1　the Bahamas：巴哈馬羣島
2　wind gust：陣風

More than 600 people died in this terrible storm. Thousands of homes were lost. Repairing the damage cost more than any other storm up till then[1].

Hurricane Mitch, 1998

Storms kill more people in poor countries. There is not enough money to build sturdy[2] houses. The people may not have phones to call for help or radios and TVs to watch for storm warnings.

Rescue services in poor countries are not as well equipped as those found today in the United States. A bad hurricane in a poor country is more likely to cause a disaster.

Hurricane Mitch hit Central America on October 29, 1998. It brought 180 mph winds and heavy rains. The rain lasted for days.

---

1   till then：至今
2   sturdy, *adj*：穩固

More than 2 feet of water fell in a single 24-hour period. Hundreds of villages were flooded. Homes and other buildings were swept away by the water. Roads and bridges were washed out. There was no way for people to escape the floods.

The hurricane left about 10,000 dead and 2 million homeless in Honduras[1], Belize[2], Nicaragua[3], and Guatemala. Many of them drowned. Others died when mudslides[4] buried their villages. The worst mudslide happened near an old volcano. Part of the crater wall[5] fell apart. An avalanche[6] of mud, rocks, and trees rolled down the mountainside onto the villages below.

A survivor told of seeing parts of dead bodies poking up[7] from the soft ground. About 1,500 people died this way. The actual number will never be known.

---

1   Honduras：洪都拉斯

2   Belize：伯利茲

3   Nicaragua：尼加拉瓜

4   mudslide, n：泥石流

5   crater wall：火口壁

6   avalanche, n：大量

7   poke up：暴露於

Naming Hurricanes

Americans started naming hurricanes in 1950 to keep track of[1] the deadly storms. The first hurricane of the year is given a name beginning with the letter A. The second is given a name beginning with B, and so on[2].

A hurricane name is "retired" if the hurricane kills many people or causes a lot of damage. That name is not used again for another hurricane. Retiring hurricane names helps avoid confusing two hurricanes with the same name.

---

1 keep track of：留意
2 and so on：如此類推

Some Retired Hurricane Names

Hurricane Camille was one of the strongest storms ever recorded. It struck land at Mississippi and Louisiana[1] in 1969. More than 250 died.

Hurricane Gilbert struck the Caribbean and Mexico in 1988. It was one of the most powerful hurricanes ever recorded.

Hurricane Hugo stormed through the Caribbean in 1989. It killed dozens[2] on several small Caribbean islands. It travelled on to the United States and struck South Carolina[3].

1　Louisiana：路易斯安那州
2　dozens, *determiner*：許多
3　South Carolina：南卡羅萊納

Hurricane Andrew was almost as powerful and destructive as Hurricane Camille. Winds of 150 mph and a 23-foot storm surge struck Eleuthera Island[1] in the Bahamas. Damage on the islands was more than $250 million.

The hurricane continued on toward Florida. It smashed ashore near Homestead, Florida, on August 24, 1992. The killer storm continued through the Gulf of Mexico to Louisiana.

Hurricane Andrew was the most costly[2] storm in American history.

---

1 Eleuthera Island：伊柳賽拉島
2 costly：代價高昂的

4 Tornadoes
如何避過龍捲風

Timeline 時間軸

March 18, 1925
The Tri-State Tornado tears through Missouri, Illinois, and Indiana.

1925 年 3 月 18 日
"三州大龍捲"撕裂密蘇里、伊利諾和印地安那三個州。

April 11, 1965
37 tornadoes hit Tornado Alley in only nine hours.

1965 年 4 月 11 日
單單九個小時內，就有37個龍捲風襲擊"龍捲風之路"。

Where is Missouri? 密蘇里州在哪裏？

MISSOURI　密蘇里州

DID YOU KNOW? 你知道嗎？

Most tornadoes in the northern hemisphere spin counter-clockwise. In the southern hemisphere, most spin clockwise.

北半球大多數龍捲風以逆時針方向轉動，而在南半球，多數是順時針。

KEY TERMS 重點詞彙

tornado - a swirling mass of winds that sucks up everything in its path

龍捲風以旋轉風形式出現，所到之處吞噬一切。

funnel - the central part of the tornado

龍捲風中央部分的漏斗雲柱。

swarm - a group of tornadoes

龍捲風羣為多枚龍捲風聚集起來。

terrorize - to fill with fear

使畏懼

Chapter Four:
Tornadoes

Tornadoes can be sudden and deadly. Most other storms form slowly. There is usually time to warn people. A tornado drops down[1] from the clouds ready to destroy everything in its path.

Darkening Clouds

It is difficult to know when or where a tornado will strike. Sometimes people see dark clouds spinning in the sky before a tornado appears. The clouds may look green as well as gray and black.

A loud roar[2] may come down from the sky, like the sound of a plane flying too close to the ground. Sometimes people see lightning in the clouds or inside the funnel of the tornado itself.

---

1   drop down：突然下來
2   a loud roar：巨大聲響

Tornadoes are smaller than hurricanes. However, they can pack more power. Size is not a good measure of a tornado's strength. A small tornado can be more powerful—and do more damage—than a large one.

Most tornadoes are quite weak. Their winds spin at about 40 mph. These tornadoes may knock over[1] a tree or a traffic sign. People can be hurt when flying objects hit them.

Violent Winds

Violent tornadoes have winds as High as 300 mph. These monster[2] tornadoes can tear houses apart. They can toss[3] cars around as if they were toys. Heavy things, like refrigerators, can become deadly missiles.

---

1   knock over：碰翻
2   monster, adj：巨大的
3   toss sth around：抛

Tornadoes disappear as suddenly as they appear. Sometimes they are gone after only a few seconds or minutes. A few tornadoes last as long as an hour or more. One of the longest tornadoes on record lasted three and a half hours. Tornadoes like that can travel as far as 100 miles.

Tornado Alley

Tornadoes can occur in many parts of the world. The United States has more tornadoes than other countries. There are about 1,000 tornadoes in the United States every year.

No place is safe from tornadoes. Big cities, like Ft. Worth, Texas, have been hit by a tornado. Even the suburbs[1] of Washington, D. C. have the occasional[2] tornado. In September 2001, two sisters were killed by a tornado. They were inside a car when the tornado whipped through the University of Maryland, near

---

1   suburb, *n*：郊區
2   occasional, *adj*：偶然出現的

Washington, D.C. The tornado picked up[1] the car and threw it around[2].

Some states in America have more Tornadoes than others. Most tornadoes happen in Tornado Alley. Tornado Alley is in the central part of the United States. It is a large area that includes many states. There are cities and small towns in Tornado Alley. There are a lot of farms, too.

Tornadoes usually happen in the spring and summer. This is when the weather is very warm and wet. There are tornadoes almost every week during this time.

Tornado Alley has about 700 tornadoes a year. Sometimes many tornadoes appear at once. These groups of tornadoes are called "swarms."

---

1 pick up：捲起
2 throw sth around：拋起轉動某物

Staying Safe

The safest place to be when a tornado hits is underground. Many houses in Tornado Alley have strong basements[1]. When people see a tornado coming, they can run into one of these shelters.

A bad place to hide is inside a car. A car is not a safe place to be when a tornado is coming.

Tri-State Tornado, March 1925

The worst tornado disaster happened in March 1925. A tornado travelled 219 miles through three Midwestern states. It became known as[2] the Tri-State Tornado.

The Tri-State Tornado was the deadliest tornado in America's history. 695 people were killed. 2,000 were injured. Houses and farms were destroyed.

1　basement, *n*：地下室
2　become known as：以…聞名

This tornado formed in the skies over Missouri. It touched down and killed 11 in that state.

Then it crossed the border into[1] Illinois. It went through the town of Gorham. The tornado killed or injured about half the people who lived or worked there.

The tornado moved on[2] through Illinois and into Indiana. It struck several mining towns along the way. Schools were torn apart[3]. Many children were killed.

The tornado went through Princeton, Indiana. Then it disappeared.

The tornado had travelled at about 62 mph. That's approximately the speed of a car on the highway. No tornado before had ever gone so fast and so far, or killed so many.

---

1   cross into：穿過
2   move on：往前走
3   tear apart：扯開

"Super Outbreak" April, 1974

Sometimes several tornadoes start at once. Over a period of two days in April 1974, 148 killer tornadoes terrorized parts of the United States and Canada.

For about six hours, a new tornado appeared every few minutes. Tornadoes were reported in 13 states and two Canadian provinces.

A mile-wide tornado ripped through[1] the large town of Xenia, Ohio. The tornado blew apart schools and churches. Stores and shops were smashed to bits.

A freight train[2] was travelling through Xenia when the tornado hit. The tornado knocked the train over, as if it were a toy.

The tornado destroyed half of the town. 33 people were killed in Xenia.10,000 people were left homeless.

---

1   rip through：迅速摧毀
2   freight train：貨運列車

Trying to help the survivors[1] was difficult because of the tornado damage. The fallen[2] train blocked the way fire trucks and ambulances needed to go.

There were also killer tornadoes in Kentucky, Indiana, Tennessee, and Alabama. Altogether, this swarm of[3] tornadoes killed more than 300 people.

---

1   survivor, *n*：生還者
2   fallen, *adj*：倒下的
3   swarm of：一大羣

Waco, Texas, 1953

A huge tornado hit the city of Waco, Texas, on May 11, 1953. It killed 114 people. About 600 more were injured. The tornado blew buildings apart. Bricks rained down on the street below. Cars and people were crushed[1]. Some survivors were rescued after being buried alive[2] for more than 12 hours.

Tornado Alley, 1965

A swarm of 37 tornadoes terrorized the people of Tornado Alley for nine hours. 271 were killed.

---

1   be crushed：被壓扁
2   be buried alive：被活埋

Snapshot

A Swarm of Tornadoes 龍捲風羣

Wichita Falls, Texas, 1979

A one-mile-wide tornado ripped through the town of Wichita Falls on April 10, 1979. It left 42 people dead and 20,000 homeless. This tornado was part of a swarm that touched down[1] in Texas and Oklahoma that day.

Kansas and Oklahoma, 1991

A swarm of tornadoes struck Kansas and Oklahoma in April 1991. It destroyed many houses and hundreds of mobile homes[2]. More than 30 people were killed. Hundreds were injured.

---

1   touch down：着陸
2   mobile home：流動房屋

Jarrell, Texas, 1997

A tornado cut through[1] the town of Jarrell on May 27, 1997. The tornado killed at least 32 people.

Arkansas and Tennessee, 1999

Swarms of tornadoes hit Arkansas and Tennessee in January 1999. 169 separate tornadoes were reported.

Oklahoma City, 1999

A swarm of more than 50 violent tornadoes[2] ripped through four states. The area around Oklahoma City was hit hard with more than $1 billion damage.

---

1 cut through：穿過
2 violent tornado：猛烈的龍捲風

Eastern States, 2002

A swarm of very powerful tornadoes ripped through the eastern United States in November 2002. Tennessee and Alabama were hard hit. Ohio, Pennsylvania, and Mississippi were also affected by the storms. Dozens of people were reported killed or missing. Some of them were rescue workers[1].

Kansas to Georgia, 2003

384 tornadoes raged through[2] 19 states during the week of May 4, 2003. This total set a new record.

---

1   rescue worker：救援人員
2   rage through：席捲

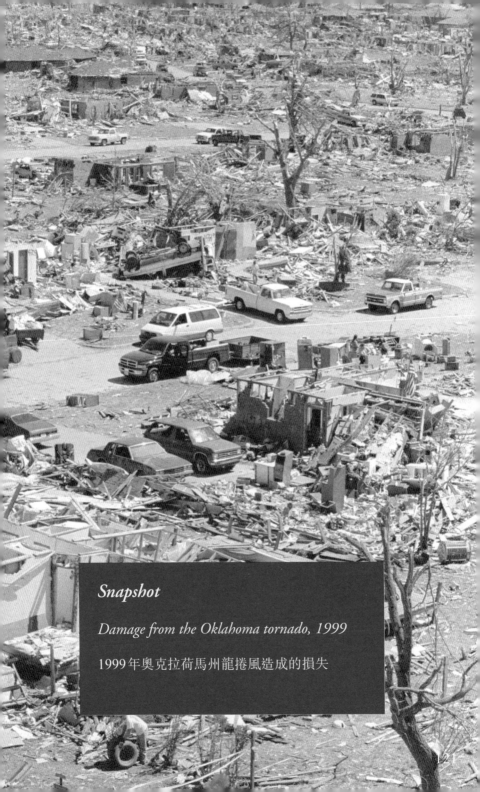

Snapshot

Damage from the Oklahoma tornado, 1999

1999年奧克拉荷馬州龍捲風造成的損失

5 The Perfect Storm
特大風暴

Timeline 時間軸

October 27, 1991

1991 年 10 月 27 日

The Halloween Storm begins as a hurricane.

萬聖節的風暴開始形成颶風。

March 12—13, 1993

1993 年 3 月 12-13 日

The Storm of the Century strikes the United States, killing more than 300 people.

這場世紀風暴侵襲美國，奪去300條人命。

Where is New England? 新英格蘭在哪裏？

NEW ENGLAND 新英格蘭

DID YOU KNOW? 你知道嗎？

Each year about 100,000 thunderstorms occur in the United States. About 10 percent of these are severe.

每年美國約發生100,000個雷暴，大概百分之十屬於嚴重。

KEY TERMS 重點詞彙

Nor'easter - a storm in New England that brings heavy rains

東北風暴是在新英格蘭形成的風暴

New England - the name given to the most northeastern states: Connecticut, Rhode Island, Massachusetts, New Hampshire, Vermont, and Maine

新英格蘭泛指美國東北各州：康乃狄格州、羅得島、馬薩諸塞州、新罕布什爾州、佛蒙特州和緬因州

Chapter Five:
The Perfect Storm

New England is used to storms called "Nor'easters." Winds blow in from the northeast. Nor'easters bring heavy rains and rough seas[1]. Nor'easters are very bad news for boats at sea.

The Halloween Storm

The "Halloween Storm" of 1991 was much worse than any nor'easter. It was the "perfect storm."

It was "perfect" because so many different things happened together[2]. The perfect storm started with Hurricane Grace. It formed on October 27, 1991.

---

1   rough sea：波濤洶湧的海
2   happen together：同時發生

Scientists watched the hurricane on their computer screens. It moved up the east coast from Bermuda. The scientists were amazed at[1] what they saw.

Several storm systems combined with[2] the hurricane. Cold air was coming down from Canada. Huge waves smashed the east coast, from North Carolina up to Nova Scotia, Canada. After a few days, the hurricane became weaker. But the Halloween Storm grew stronger.

The Halloween Storm killed six fishermen on the boat, *Andrea Gail.* Their story was turned into[3] a book and a movie, both called *The Perfect Storm.*

The Halloween storm killed others, too. Two men drowned off Staten Island, New York, when their boat turned over[4] in the storm.

---

1   amaze at：感到驚訝
2   combine with：與…結合
3   turn into：改作
4   turn over：翻倒

Most people know how dangerous it is to be near the shore during a big storm. Some people ignore the danger and pay with their lives.

A man in Rhode Island was fishing during the storm. Big waves washed him off the rocks and he drowned. The storm killed a man in New York who was fishing from a bridge. He was either blown off the bridge by the strong winds or swept away by the water.

The storm caused a lot of damage. Homes and businesses in New England were ruined[1]. Land near the coast was flooded. Roads and airports were forced to[2] close.

Finally, the Halloween Storm got weaker. As the perfect storm died, a new hurricane formed at its center.

---

1   ruin, *v*：破壞
2   be forced to：被迫

Since 1950, almost all hurricanes have been named. This new hurricane was an exception[1]. It never received a name.

There was a good reason for[2] this. People were still talking about the Halloween Storm. Naming the new hurricane might confuse them.

The no-name hurricane blew out to sea. The Halloween Storm was over.

---

1   exception, *n*：例外
2   a good reason for：合理原因

Snapshot

This scene from the movie The Perfect Storm shows the boat in the crashing waves created by the storm.

電影〈地動天搖〉的其中一幕，顯示遇到風暴，投入洶湧怒濤中的船。

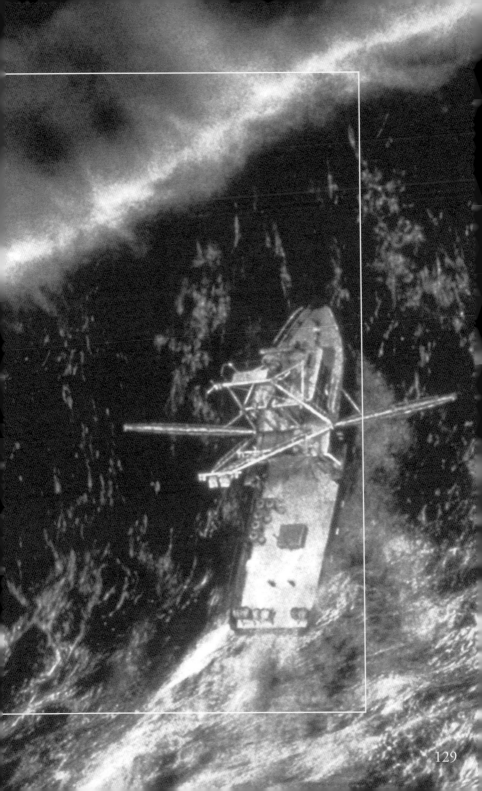

"Storm of the Century"

In March 1993, a huge storm closed down[1] the east coast of the United States for several days. It was called "The Storm of the Century."

Tornadoes, high winds, and very heavy snows stretched from[2] Florida up to the Northeast. 44 people were killed by a swarm of tornadoes in Florida. Wind speeds reached 100 mph.

The storm blew down trees and power lines. Millions of people had no electricity in their homes. Roads and airports were closed. Snow fell on parts of the southern United States that almost never get snow.

---

1   close down：封鎖
2   stretch from...to...：由…延伸至…

Farther north[1], the snow fell at a rate of about 2 to 3 inches an hour. Some places got more than 3 feet of snow.

The storm claimed 270 lives[2] on land. 48 people were missing at sea. It cost billions of dollars to repair the damage caused by the Storm of the Century.

1　farther north：更遠的北面
2　claim...lives：導致…人死亡

6 StormReady
及時發出警告

StormReady is a National Weather Service program. StormReady helps communities plan for[1], and deal with, deadly storms.

A community must do many things before it is StormReady. For example, it must have a 24-hour warning point and emergency operations centre.

In November 2002, a tornado hit Van Wert County, Ohio. The StormReady warning alert system in a movie theater went off. More than 50 people escaped.

Only minutes later, a tornado whipped through the building. It hurled[2] cars into the movie screen and onto the seats.

This is one example of StormReady's success. The National Weather Service hopes to save more lives with the Storm Ready system. For more facts, see: http://www.stormready.noaa.gov/index.html

---

1   plan for：為…做安排
2   hurl, *v*：猛投

Exercises 練習

1   Vocabulary 詞彙

1.1 Self-Assessment 自我評估

以下詞彙跟各種風暴有關，在這些詞彙下畫上底線。

1. meteorologist
2. surge
3. tropical cyclone
4. cyclone shelter
5. hurricane
6. eye
7. mudslide
8. tornado
9. funnel
10. swarm
11. terrorize
12. Nor'easter

1.2 Words to Know 認識生詞

請配對：

1. mph＿＿＿＿＿
2. priority＿＿＿＿
3. violent＿＿＿＿
4. severe＿＿＿＿
5. gust＿＿＿＿＿

A. acting with great force
B. something that comes first because of its importance
C. a strong, sudden rush of wind
D. miles per hour
E. very strong

1.3 Word Ladders 字梯

按提示改詞語的一個字母，使它變成下一個詞語，請見示範。

calm	peace
a certain area	place
a flat dish	＿＿＿＿

writing tablet of stone   _____
to say   _____
to look directly   _____
a place to buy goods   _____
strong winds and heavy rain   _____

---

wet earth   mud
something that doesn't work   dud
owe as payment   _____
to colour material or hair   _____
sailor's "yes"   _____
card that stands for one   _____
frozen water   _____

---

prepared   ready
small, round, and shiny   beady
bends easily   _____
curves   _____
to tie with rope   _____
discovers   _____
payments as punishments   _____
more than one 5   _____
living beings   _____

---

water from the sky   rain
a surprise attack   raid
stated aloud   _____
tiny grains of rock   _____
a stick used by a magician   _____
moving air   _____

2   Initial Understanding 初步理解

2.1 True or False? 是非題

細讀以下句子，看那一句對，那一句錯。

1. Topical storms occur only in the tropics.　　T　F

2. Now, scientists can always predict storms.　　T　F

3. Tornadoes always last only a few minutes.　　T　F

4. Cyclones are tropical cyclones that begin in the Indian Ocean.　　T　F

5. Floods from storms can kill plants as well as people and animals.　　T　F

6. A cyclone shelter protects people with its strong walls.　　T　F

7. Hurricanes are like strong thunderstorms.　　T　F

8. The eye of the storm is where it is most violent.　　T　F

9. Tornado Alley is where people go to be safe from tornadoes.　　T　F

10. A Nor'easter is a famous storm that happened on Easter 1991.　　T　F

3 Reflection 思考

3.1 Similes and Metaphors 明喻和隱喻

A simile（明喻）用 like 或 as 連接兩種不同事物。A metaphor（隱喻）連接兩種不同事物，但不用 like 或 as。

以下句子含可比較詞彙，在它們之下畫底線，並寫出兩者相似之處。請見示範。

1. The <u>flood</u> was like a <u>blanket smothering the earth</u>.
   Both the flood and the blanket cover the land completely and don't let air get through.
2. The swarm of tornadoes was a swarm of angry bees.

Answer Key 答案

Part 1
Air Disasters

1.1 Word Ladders

head, heal, teal, tell, tall, tail
fog, foe, doe, dye, aye, ace, ice
gas, has, his, sis, sir, air
blind, bland, brand, brans, beans,
beaks, peaks

1.2 Making Connections

possible answers: 'head and tail'
can both relate to wind direction.
'fog and ice' are both weather
conditions that may cause air
disasters.
'gas and air' were used for airships.
'blind and peaks' was a sequence
for an air disaster in Chile. The
pilot was flying blind. He thought
he was landing at the airport, but
he landed on mountain peaks.

2.1 Read for Details

1. Ch 1 People could first buy a
plane ticket in 1952.
2. Ch 1, 2, 3, 4 Pilots can fly blind
by using the plane's computer,
radar, information from the control
tower, and a compass.
3. Ch 4 Planes can be de-iced
with machines used to melt ice
at airports and with anti-icing
equipment in the plane itself.
4. Ch 6 On September 11, 2001, no
planes flew so that there would be

no more hijacks.
5. Ch 2 A plane ran into another
one when it was trying to take off
from the Canary Islands.
6. Ch 1 Using helium gas might
have made the Hindenburg safe
from fire.
7. Ch 3 No one could see the white
plane because it blended in with
the snow.
8. Ch 5 The passenger planes were
off course and over restricted air
space.
9. Ch 3 Two survivors walked to a
village, 10 days away to get help.
10. Ch 4 Survivors were rescued
by helicopter rather than by boat.

3.1 Flow Charts

Sample answers:
The pilot wanted to show the
passengers a close
view of Mt. Erebus.
The pilot lowered the plane.
The plane crashed into the volcano.

3.2 Sequence of Events

Sample paragraph: The left engine
came off a plane in Chicago right
before take-off. Then the pilot tried
to go back and land after take-off.
Next the plane crashed into the
ground close to the runway. After
that, the plane exploded and plane
parts fell in a mobile park. A fire
broke out in the park. In the end,
everyone on the plane and 2 people
in the mobile park were killed.

137

Part 2
Deadly Storms

1.1 Self-Assessment

Underlined words: tropical cyclone, hurricane,
tornado, Nor'easter

1.2 Words To Know

1. D; 2. B; 3. A; 4. E; 5. C

1.3 Word Ladders

peace, place, plate, slate, state, stare, store, storm
mud, dud, due, dye, aye, ace, ice
ready, beady, bendy, bends, binds, finds, fines, fives, lives
rain, raid, said, sand, wand, wind

2.1 True or False?

1. F; 2. F; 3. F; 4. T; 5. T; 6. F; 7. T; 8. F; 9. F; 10. F

3.1 Similes and Metaphors

Sample responses include:
1. underlined: flood, blanket smothering the earth. Both the flood and the blanket cover the land completely and don't let air get through.
2. underlined: swarm of tornadoes, swarm of angry bees. Angry bees are powerful and dangerous, just like tornadoes.

Proper names
專有名詞

Andes Mountains
安第斯山脈

Bangladesh
孟加拉（內地譯：孟加拉
人民共和國）

blizzards
暴風雪

Canessa, Roberto
卡涅薩
（烏拉圭橄欖球員）

Carribbean, the
加勒比海

Chile
智利

Galveston, Texas
加爾維斯敦
（美國德克薩斯州
東南部港市）

Hindenburg
興登堡號飛船

Lakehurst
雷克赫斯特

Nando, Parrado
南度（烏拉圭橄欖球員）

Pentagon
五角大廈

Perez, Marcelo
培瑞斯
（烏拉圭橄欖球隊隊長）

Perfect Storm, the
特大風暴

Storm of the Century
世紀風暴

Tenerife
特內里費島
（內地又譯：特納里夫）

Tornado Alley
龍捲風走廊

Washington, D. C.
首都華盛頓

World Trade Centre
世界貿易中心

Nando, Parrado
南度
（烏拉圭橄欖球員）

Pentagon
五角大廈

Perez, Marcelo
培瑞斯（烏拉圭橄欖球隊
隊長）

General
Vocabulary
一般詞彙

a chain of
一連串的

air traffic
航空交通

amaze at
感到驚訝

anti-icing
防冰

as well as
也

at risk
有危險

aviation
航空

basement
地下室

become known as
以…聞名

blend in
與…和諧

blimp
小飛艇

blizzard
暴風雪

block the sun
擋住太陽

BOAC
英國海外航空公司

break up
解體

cargo area
貨運區

charter
租

clean up
清理

close down
封鎖

combine with
與…結合

congressman
國會議員

commercial airplanes
商用航機

cyclones
大旋風

cross into
穿過

crumble
碎成細屑

crush
壓扁

deadlier
傷亡更嚴重

deadly mistake
致命錯誤

de-iced
除冰的

different from
異於…

dip down
落下

dramatic
激動人心的

drop down
突然下來

exception
例外

emergency landing
緊急降落

equator
赤道

equip
裝備

eventually
最終

extraordinary
特別的

fallen
倒下的

false alarm
虛報

farther north
更遠的北面

fire
火

flight path
飛行路徑

floods
洪水

fog
霧

fire truck
救火車

fighter plane
戰機

fly in
乘…飛行

fly over
飛到另一個地方去

force to
被迫

freight train
貨運列車

hang onto life
掙扎求存

happen together
同時發生

head for
朝…進發

headquarter
總部

helium gas
氦氣

hijack
劫持

hit
襲擊

homeless
無家可歸的

hop over
躍過

huddle
蜷縮身體

hundreds of
許許多多

hurl
猛投

hurricane
颶風

ice
冰

infant
嬰孩

in time
及時

good reaen for
合理原因

keep going
繼續運行

knock over
碰翻

leave sb homeless
令人無家可歸

lifesavers
救生者

lift off
起飛

lightning
閃電

live with
容忍

locate on
位於…之上

look down on
俯瞰

magnetic pole
磁極

meteo rdogist
氣象學家

mechanical failure
機件故障

meteorologist
氣象學者

mudslide
泥流

missile
導彈

mobile home
活動房屋

monster
巨大的

mountaintop
山頂

move on
往前走

no matter what
無論甚麼

off course
偏離原定的航程

on fire
起火

on high alert
提高警惕

140

opening 缺口	shelters 遮蔽	the Department of Defence 國防部
ordeal 苦難	skim over 滑過	throw sth around 拋起轉動某物
overhead 在空中	slam into 猛烈撞擊	thunderstorm 雷暴
pass ove 經過	slush 半融雪	tornadoes 龍捲風
pick up 拾起	smash off 粉碎	tropical cyclone 熱帶氣旋
pile up 堆積	snap off 折斷	tropical storms 熱帶風暴
plan for 為…做安排	spin around 圍繞…旋轉	toss into 扔進
plough 翻起	starve to death 餓死	tragic result 悲劇後果
point to 顯示真相	struggle 拼搏	turbulence 氣流
program sb's route 為某人的路線編寫程式	stuck in 陷入	turn into 改作
pull into 進入	storm surge 風暴潮	turn into a nightmare 變成惡夢
...raised 加高	suburb 郊區	turn over 翻倒
return to 恢復	suck up 吸取	U. S. Capitol building 美國國會大廈
ridge 山脊	surge 奔湧向前	under attack 受到攻擊
rip 扯破	survivor 生還者	unpredictable 捉摸不透的
rip through 迅速摧毀	suspicious of 懷疑	vest 背心
rough sea 波濤洶湧的海	sweep away 一掃而空	violent tornado 猛烈的龍捲風
ruin 破壞	tail wind 順風	visibility 視程
runway 跑道	take off from 以…為出發點	walk off 離開
scatter 散佈	takeoff 起飛	warship 軍艦
seat cover 座椅套	taxi down 滑行	whip around 轉過身來
scrap 廢棄	tear apart 扯開	work together 共同合作
severed 已分離的	terrorism 恐怖主義	wreckage 殘片

Brennan, Kristine. *The Galveston Hurricane*. Great Disasters, Reforms and Ramifications. Philadelphia: Chelsea House Publishers, 2002.

Byers, Ann. *The Crash of the Concorde*. When Disaster Strikes! New York: Rosen Central, 2003.

Challoner, Jack. *Hurricane & Tornado*. DK Eyewitness Books. New York: Dorling Kindersley Pub., 2000.

Friedrich, Belinda. *The Explosion of TWA Flight 800*. Great Disasters, Reforms and Ramifications. Philadelphia: Chelsea House Publishers, 2002.

Gaffney, Timothy R. *Air Safety: Preventing Future Disasters*. Issues in Focus. Springfield, NJ: Enslow, 1999.

Hirschmann, Kris. *Hurricanes*. Natural Disasters. San Diego: Lucent Books, 2002.

Kling, Andrew A. *Tornadoes*. Natural Disasters. San Diego: Lucent Books, 2002.

Landau, Elaine. *Air Crashes*. Watts Library. New York: Franklin Watts, 1999.

Majoor, Mireille. *Inside the Hindenburg*. Boston: Little, Brown and Company, 2000.